RED MULE

RED MULE

Jesse Stuart

Edited By
JERRY A. HERNDON

Original Illustrations
ROBERT HENNEBERGER

THE JESSE STUART FOUNDATION
Ashland, Kentucky
1993

Dedicated to
**The Honorable Order
of Kentucky Colonels**

The Jesse Stuart Foundation
RED MULE

Copyright© 1955 by Jesse Stuart
Copyright© 1983 by The Jesse Stuart Foundation

Library of Congress Cataloging - in - Publication Data

Stuart, Jesse, date
  Red Mule, / Jesse Stuart ; edited by Jerry A. Herndon ;
original illustrations, Robert Henneberger.
     p. cm.
  Summary: Working to save the mules in their Kentucky
community from being butchered at the cannery, twelve-
year-old Scrappie and his friend Red Mule see their cause
vindicated when tractors get stuck in the river mud and
only mules can pull them out.
  ISBN 0-945084-34-X : $12.00. -- ISBN 0-945084-33-1 : $6.00
  [1. Mules--Fiction. 2. Kentucky--Fiction.] I. Herndon,
Jerry A. II. Henneberger, Robert, ill. III. Title.
PZ7. S937Re 1993
[Fic]--dc20   92-31439
                                                        CIP
                                                        AC

Published by:
The Jesse Stuart Foundation
P.O. Box 391 Ashland, KY 41114
1993

Table of Contents

Red Mule Has a Helper

Red Mule stood under the leafy elm and watched Scrappie as he drove the span of big mules hitched to a disk harrow across the lot to the shade. The mules were getting wet with perspiration and Scrappie knew how much the mules could stand. He had been working mules for almost two years now. When Scrappie drove them toward the elm, the big man waited for him with a smile on his face.

"Scrappie," Red Mule said, "you're going to make a great teamster. You like mules. And when you like them, they like you. I've liked mules since I was so small I had to stand up in the barn mangers to fasten the collars around their necks. You're just like I was when I was twelve years old. You're the only boy left around here who likes mules."

"Gee, Red Mule, I'm proud of what you've said to me," Scrappie told him.

Scrappie sat on the springy seat of the disk harrow with the leather check lines in his hand. His face was tanned by the spring wind and sun. He didn't wear a hat and his black hair was tousled by the wind.

"You taught me to like mules," he said.

Scrappie smiled as he watched Red Mule put his big hand on Dick's back to wipe off the loose hair he was shedding for spring.

Just then Milford Royster drove his tractor into the big field across the street. This field held four garden lots. When Red Mule saw him driving in, he stopped rubbing the loose hairs from Dick's back. He watched Milford set his plows down and start his tractor around the first lot. The two plows were turning the dark dirt over fast. The tractor engine sang a song Red Mule and Scrappie didn't like to hear. Red Mule plugged his ears with his big index fingers. Scrappie looked toward the tractor and the smile left his face. Dick and Dinah snorted, but they stood quietly. They didn't like to hear the noise the tractor engine made, either.

"Do you reckon old Milford likes his tractor as much as we like our mules?" Red Mule asked Scrappie. He talked loud so Scrappie could hear him over the noise of the tractor.

"I don't see how he could," Scrappie replied. "The tractor can't put its mouth on his shoulder and nibble when it wants something. The tractor can't talk to him."

"So you've learned mules can talk," Red Mule said with a big grin that showed the mouthful of big teeth behind his red beard. "When you're sure they talk, that's when you fall in love with them and they fall in love with you." Red Mule spoke more softly now, for the tractor was on the back side of the lot. "You'll be a real mule man when you grow up. People around here will be calling you Mule, too. Only you don't have red hair like I have, so they might call you Young Mule. Then they might start calling me Old Mule instead of Red Mule. You'll be Young Mule and I'll be Old Mule. Listen to that awful tractor!" The tractor had circled back again and its harsh song was louder. But Dick and Dinah, a fine-looking pair of big mules, stood very quietly on the soft ground. The only time either raised a foot or swished a tail was when he was bitten by a bluetail fly. Dick and Dinah didn't like flies. Scrappie didn't either. When one of the flies came around, he got off the harrow and caught it. Red Mule had shown him how to do this. Scrappie would ease up close and then slap his hand over the fly. He'd gotten so good at it he never missed.

"Red Mule, I believe mules can understand our talk, too," Scrappie said. "Old Dick and Dinah are listening right now to what we're saying about them."

"Sure, they're listening," Red Mule agreed. "Mules have a way of listening to what is said about them. That's the reason many men are kicked by mules. A man has to be awfully mean to say anything bad about a mule. If he does, he deserves to be kicked!"

"I've worked Dick and Dinah long enough that I believe they can understand me, and I know I can understand them," Scrappie said. "I can't tell this to my father and mother and a lot of other people. They wouldn't believe me!" Scrappie had to shout, for Milford was circling back around with his tractor. "But now I know they can. And I'd rather hear mules than a tractor any time!"

"When Milford first got that tractor," Red Mule told Scrappie, "I said to myself, 'It's goin' to be hard on me and my mules. There might even come a time when we won't get enough to eat!' I saw right then, Scrappie, hard times were coming, and I've been plowing lots around this town for over thirty years. I could see I had trouble, Scrappie!"

"Do you think we're going to lose out?" Scrappie asked, looking up at the big man.

"I don't know, Scrappie," Red Mule said with a frown as he watched Milford start around another lot on his tractor. "He can plow four lots while we're plowing one. He has really hurt our business with that thing! I used to plow all the lots in Blakesburg and now I don't get a fourth of the spring gardens and truck patches to plow."

"That's all right, Red Mule," Scrappie said. "We'll fight for the business!"

"Yes, the tractors are hurting us," Red Mule continued. "But I still think there's a place in the world for mules. I think this country has a great need for mules!"

"Look, he's going to finish plowing and disking those four lots before we get one plowed and disked," Scrappie sighed.

"Let' im go," Red Mule said. "Let' im do it. You give Dick and Dinah their time. They might be slow compared to that tractor but they get there just the same. Just don't rush these mules and try to do as much as Milford's tractor can."

"I won't, Red Mule," Scrappie told him. "You've always taught me that if I let the mules stay in their own gait, they will be very slow to tire."

"You're a lot lighter on that disk than I am," Red Mule said. "I'm too much of a load for the mules to pull on a disk that cuts deep in plowed ground. So you go on, Scrappie."

"Get up, Dick and Dinah!" Scrappie called, shaking the lines in his hands. "You've had a good rest now. Let's make another round or two before dinnertime!"

Scrappie spoke to them just like Red Mule. He used the same words that Red Mule used. The mules stepped briskly, pulling the heavy disk harrow through the soft ground. Scrappie sat up proudly on the seat with the leather check lines in his hands, just as he had seen Red Mule sit up proudly on his wagon as he was driving Dick and Dinah through Blakesburg.

As Red Mule watched Scrappie driving the big mule team, he smiled. But when he turned to look across the street at Milford Royster, the smile left his face. "We'd better quit for dinner, Scrappie!" he called.

Scrappie drove the mules over to the elm shade and stopped them. Then Red Mule walked

over and unhitched Dinah while Scrappie unhitched Dick. They unhooked the trace chains
and wrapped them around the back bands. Each
folded a leather check line up in a bundle and tied
it with the end of the line and hung it over a hame
above the mule's collar. Red Mule led Dinah over
to the wagon, and Scrappie followed with Dick.
Here Red Mule poured feed from a sack into the
feedboxes.

"I'll water them before you get back,
Scrappie," Red Mule said.

"Where's your dinner, Red Mule?" Scrappie
asked, looking into the wagon.

"I didn't bring any today," the big man replied.

"But won't you get hungry?" Scrappie asked.

Red mule looked at Scrappie and grinned.
"Oh, sometimes I do," he said. "But shucks, I
ain't done much work this morning. You and
Dick and Dinah have done the work. I've just
stood around and watched you and Milford and
his tractor."

"But you'll get hungry, Red Mule," Scrappie
said. "Come home with me and eat!"

Scrappie invited Red Mule before he thought.
Suddenly he hoped Red Mule wouldn't accept his
invitation, because he had heard his mother talk
so much about Red Mule being dirty. He'd also
heard his mother's friends say they had to stop

breathing when they passed Red Mule on the street because he smelled bad. But Scrappie knew better, and he had tried to explain to his mother that the smell on Red Mule wasn't caused by dirt. He knew what kind of smell it was. It was mule smell.

Red Mule stood there looking at Scrappie, trying to make up his mind whether to go or not. Then he said, "I'd better not go today. Thank you, Scrappie!"

When Scrappie had walked a few steps, he turned to look back. Red Mule didn't see him looking, and he saw Red Mule dip his hand into the feedbox and come up with a handful of feed.

Scrappie watched Red Mule take a big bite of the feed from his hand, then brush the crumbs from his whiskers. He knew Red Mule was hungry. Scrappie was hungry, too, but as he walked toward his home his hunger went away. He felt bad about Red Mule not having anything to eat.

Scrappie's Mother Has a Guest

"Wash your hands and face now, Scrappie!" his mother called just as he walked up on the porch. "You're late!"

"Mom, I'll wash my face and hands, but I'm not hungry," Scrappie answered.

His pretty mother, Mary Lykins, looked very closely at her son. She thought he might be sick. He always came home hungry when he worked with Red Mule. He and his mother always ate lunch together. His father ate at the Dinner Bell, a restaurant down the street from his grocery store. His father could take only a few minutes for lunch.

"What's the matter with you, Scrappie?" his mother asked him, with concern in her voice. "Are you sick?"

"No, Mom, I'm not sick," he replied.

"Did something go wrong?" she asked him.

"Mom, poor old Red Mule hasn't any lunch!"

"Well, he could have, couldn't he?" she said, looking at Scrappie with her soft blue eyes. "He gets paid for every garden he plows, doesn't he? And he's never paid you anything for helping him. He's promised you, I know, but has he ever paid you?"

"He's got his mules to feed, Mom," Scrappie replied. "He doesn't get as many gardens to plow as he used to. Milford Royster gets them to plow with his tractor. Jed Warnock and Sylvester Lybrooks have got tractors, too, and they're getting to plow some of the gardens around here. Everybody who gets a tractor hurts Red Mule. He's had a hard winter because he didn't get much work to do. I don't care whether he pays me or not!"

His mother didn't frown, but Scrappie thought she was going to. She wasn't a bit pleased with what Scrappie had said.

"Come on now, and eat your lunch," she told him. "It's going to get cold."

"Mom, I can't eat when I know Red Mule is hungry," Scrappie said.

"How do you know he's hungry?" she asked.

"I saw him take a handful of feed from Dick's box when I looked back," he said, with tears welling up in his eyes. "A man has to be hungry to eat horse-and-mule feed!"

"But he's so. . . ."

"He's not that dirty, Mom!" Scrappie interrupted. "I work with Red Mule and I know. I
know he smells like a hot mule and he walks like
a tired one. But I like mule smell!"

"Maybe I've got enough cooked for both of
you," Mrs. Lykins told Scrappie. "Go tell him to
come over and eat with you."

Scrappie jumped up from the table and wiped
the tears from his eyes with the back of his hand.
He was smiling when he ran out the door. He
didn't take time to go down one step at a time.

He jumped all the way and took off running down the street. He ran until he reached Red Mule, standing beside the wagon watching Dick and Dinah.

"Red Mule, I've got good news!" Scrappie cried. "Mom wants you to come over to our house and eat with me today!"

"That's wonderful, Scrappie," Red Mule said. "But I ain't hungry."

"I know you are, too, Red Mule," Scrappie said. "Now, come on. If you don't, I'll stop working for you!" The big man looked surprised.

"Then I'll go along," he told Scrappie. "I don't want you to stop working for me, because you like mules. You'll make the greatest mule man around here one of these days."

Big Red Mule and little Scrappie walked away together while Dick and Dinah ate contentedly from the feedboxes in the wagon.

Red Mule took his big black hat off just as he stepped up on the porch. Scrappie started through the door and Red Mule followed him.

"Ouch!" Red Mule groaned.

"What's the matter, Red Mule?" Scrappie asked, as he turned around to see.

"I bumped my head," the big man said. "Shucks, that's not anything unusual!"

"How tall are you, Red Mule?" Scrappie asked.

"I don't know exactly," he answered. "I

haven't measured in a long time. But I 'spect I'm about six feet four, maybe six feet six."

"Bend over and watch the doors," Scrappie warned him. "Don't bump your head again. The door into the breakfast nook might be lower than this one."

Red Mule followed Scrappie through the living room, where he walked slowly and looked at the nice furniture, the starched white window curtains, and the flowered rug beneath his feet. This house was very strange to him. He'd never been in a home this nice since his mother had died, many years before. Red Mule stooped for another door, and followed Scrappie into the dining room, where his head touched the chandelier and the little glass beads rattled. The big man looked at the wallpaper, the chest, the big cupboard, and the long table in this room. On the wall was a picture of fruit that made him really hungry.

"Watch this door, Red Mule," Scrappie said.

Red Mule stooped and then turned his shoulders sideways so he could get through.

"Gee, Red Mule, I didn't know you were so big!" Scrappie exclaimed. "No wonder you don't ride the disk! I'll bet you live in a house with high doors!"

"Well, I guess you would call the doors to my house pretty high," he laughed.

"Red Mule, you've never met Mom," Scrappie

said. "This is my mother."

"I'm Mary Lykins," she said, looking up at big Red Mule.

Scrappie looked at his small, pretty mother. When Red Mule reached his big hand out, she reached her little hand out timidly, and when Red Mule had shaken her hand, she pulled it back quickly, almost as if she were afraid.

"Mrs. Lykins, I've seen you before, but I didn't know you were Scrappie's mother," Red Mule said as he looked down at the small table filled with food. "I know your husband, Frank, very well."

"Scrappie and I always eat our lunch in this breakfast nook," she said. "I hope you'll find room enough to be comfortable."

"Oh, I'll be all right, Mrs. Lykins," Red Mule said. His head was just under the ceiling. "There's plenty of room in here."

The little table was filled with food. Scrappie sat down on one side and Red Mule on the other.

"I've not fixed anything extra, since I didn't know anyone was coming," Mrs. Lykins said. "But I hope there'll be enough of what we have."

"You have plenty here for us, Mrs. Lykins," Red Mule said as he squeezed between the table and the wall. "Scrappie wanted me to come home and eat with 'im. Scrappie's goin' to make a wonderful mule man. The mules like him, and he likes them."

"Yes, I know a lot about Dick and Dinah," she said with a smile. "Now, Scrappie, you and Red Mule can help yourselves to the food. I'll leave you alone." Mrs. Lykins left the room.

Scrappie was really hungry now and he started reaching and helping himself. Red Mule's long arms could reach across the little table and beyond. He towered over the table as old Dick or Dinah would have, if they had been sitting in chairs and eating from this table. He had to spread his legs out under the table right past Scrappie's chair. If he'd pulled them up, his knees would have lifted the little table off the floor.

Red Mule was soon helping himself to the ham and eggs. He put four of the eight fried eggs on his plate. Then he helped himself to several slices of ham.

"Mom put some extras on the table while I went back to get you," Scrappie told Red Mule. "I guess she thought she didn't have enough for a couple of mule drivers like us!"

"That's it, Scrappie," Red Mule said as he put the loaded fork through his beard to his mouth.

Once the door opened and Mrs. Lykins came in. "Are you getting along all right?" she asked. "Is there enough for two hungry men?"

"Plenty, ma'am," Red Mule answered.

"Are you getting along all right, Scrappie?"

"Yes, Mom," he replied. "We're hungry and

this is a wonderful lunch."

"If you need me, Scrappie, call me," she told him.

"All right, Mom," he said. "But Red Mule and I are getting along fine."

She turned and left the breakfast nook.

"It was a fine meal," Red Mule said as he pushed his chair back and got up from the table. He stood and looked at the white curtains, but did not touch them. "I guess we'd better be getting back to Dick and Dinah," he said. "They've had a good rest."

Red Mule Sees a Way Out

"Scrappie, you lead Dick to the water hole and I'll take Dinah," Red Mule said. "You know where we have to take them to water."

"It's funny about mules," Scrappie remarked. "Can you tell me why it is they wade up and down a creek and smell the water? Then they find a place where they want to drink. If Dick and Dinah can't get back to this hole, they won't drink any place in Town Branch. They'll do without water until they get home."

"Scrappie, that's what I've always told you," Red Mule said softly as they led the big mules down a little-used, unpaved street toward the branch. "Mules are smart. Now if you had to drink from Town Branch and could select the place, wouldn't you choose the place Dick and Dinah did? It's a nice, clean hole of deep blue water and it's under the shade of big overhanging willows that keep it cool."

"I never thought about it that way, Red Mule, but you're right," Scrappie said. "Dick and Dinah are smart."

The big man and the small boy led the mules down to Town Branch. Here the street turned into a country road which dipped down and crossed the stream. There wasn't any bridge. As they walked down to the water, a cloud of early-spring butterflies rose up from the sand. The butterflies were so thick Scrappie and Red Mule had to wait for them to scatter on the wind. They rose up like a fluttering cloud of many colors and thinned on the bright April wind. Then Scrappie and Red Mule left the road and led the mules up the stream toward the grove of willows, whose leafy tops were green clouds resting on the wind.

As they led the mules upstream to the deep hole of clean, blue water, they had to walk fast because Dick and Dinah took longer steps, getting close to Red Mule's and Scrappie's heels. When they got to the water hole, they stepped out of the way and let the mules get to the water. Dick and Dinah waded to their knees while Scrappie and Red Mule held the bridle reins and watched them put their mouths down into the water and start drinking. They made a little noise as they quenched their thirst.

After they had taken Dick and Dinah back

and hitched them to the disk harrow, Scrappie climbed up onto the seat.

"We'll get this lot finished this afternoon," Red Mule said. "I can't collect until the lots have been plowed, harrowed, and the rows laid off."

"Get up, Dick and Dinah!" Scrappie said proudly. He looked small sitting on the big disk harrow seat, with the check lines in his hands. "We'll take our time, but we must get done this afternoon so Red Mule can collect!"

The mules stepped along at their slow pace. As they moved the heavy disk harrow across the lot, it ground the big clods almost as fine as sand. Before the afternoon was half over, Red Mule scooped up a big handful of the dark dirt and let it sift through his fingers. He grinned as he brushed the last grains of dirt from his big hands. Then he walked across the street to see what kind of plowing and disking Milford Royster had done for Ike Abrams.

He walked around the edge of the ground Milford had plowed. Then he walked out into the plowed earth. "Scrappie!" he called.

"Yes, Red Mule?" Scrappie answered as he reined his mules to a stop.

"Come over here a minute!" Red Mule shouted. "I want to show you something!"

Scrappie drove Dick and Dinah back to the shade of the elm tree and fastened the check lines onto the seat. Then he ran across the road to where Red Mule was standing in the middle of one of the lots Milford had plowed and harrowed.

"Won't they get us for trespassing?" Scrappie asked. "We'll pack that plowed ground down by walking over it."

"We can't hurt this ground!" Red Mule told him. "Come on!"

Red Mule had the biggest grin on his face Scrappie had ever seen. He was showing all of his teeth now. The long red hair on his head blew out behind him like a long red streamer when he took his hat off, and the April wind pressed the long red beard down against his face.

"Look, Scrappie!" Red Mule said in a loud voice, then laughed louder than the blowing wind. "Come look at this dirt! See how Milford leaves it! Does this look like soft garden dirt where Ike can plant his peas, corn, and potatoes? How can Ike ever make a lettuce bed in this kind of dirt? How can he sow radish, carrot, and beet seeds in ground like this?"

Scrappie looked at the coarse lumps of dirt in Red Mule's hand. There were three clods as big as lumps of coal.

"Looks like that ground was plowed wet," Scrappie said.

"Plowed wet, my red whiskers!" Red Mule answered. "Old Milford was in too big a hurry to get to the next lot! He missed these clods with his

disk. We might get this job to do over! Milford is in a big hurry to get all the lots and to squeeze me and the mules out! He wants all the work. He wants to starve me out. He's bragged that he'd send me to the poorhouse!"

"This ground is not half worked," Scrappie said as he stooped down and tried to lift a big clod. "How can Milford Royster do this to people? How can he get by with it?"

"Scrappie, we wouldn't get even one lot to plow if we did a job like this!" Red Mule said. "You know we wouldn't! Look all the way around beside this fence, Scrappie! Look, there's a four-foot strip that's not plowed at all. Maybe Milford was afraid of getting his tractor scratched on the fence! We wouldn't leave that much ground. That's why we bring the little plow and use one mule when we plow up close to the fence. I was worried up until now, for I thought Milford was really going to send me to the poorhouse. Now I know he's not!"

Red Mule threw the big clods up over the top of a maple and they came down and hit more clods, but didn't break. Then he laughed louder than any wind Scrappie had heard blowing up this street since winter. He laughed louder than Dick and Dinah ever brayed. He picked up more clods and threw them into the leaves on the big tree.

"What's the matter over there?" someone

called.

"Is Red Mule having some sort of fit?" Scrappie knew the voice. He turned to look as Red Mule heaved the big clods up into the leafy maple.

Mrs. Ezra Williams had stopped just across the street. She was a close friend of Scrappie's mother. He knew she would go straight home and tell his mother. She was one of the women who walked on the far side of the street when they met Red Mule.

"Oh, no, Mrs. Williams, Red Mule is all right!" Scrappie replied. "There's not anything wrong with him! He's throwing at something up in that tree!"

"I don't see anything up there for him to throw at," she said. "If you were my son, I'd be more particular about who you loaf with! I don't understand your mother sometimes!"

Mrs. Williams hurried on down the street toward Scrappie's home, as Red Mule heaved more big clods up into the tree. Red Mule was laughing and Scrappie picked up smaller clods and threw them up and laughed, too.

That afternoon when Scrappie finished harrowing, Red Mule hitched Dinah to the little single-shovel plow he used for laying off the rows. Scrappie set stakes at each end of the lot while Red Mule and Dinah laid off the rows. When he had finished, the rows were straight as ramrods.

Then Red Mule and Scrappie lifted the single-shovel plow and the big turning plow up into the wagon and chained the disk behind.

"Now hitch the team to the wagon while I go collect," Red Mule said.

The big man went across the street to Fain Meadows' home, and Scrappie started hitching up. When Red Mule returned a little while later, there was a big smile on his face, and Scrappie knew he had his pay. Scrappie was sitting up on the seat, with the mules hitched and ready to go. Dick and Dinah were prancing as if they hadn't worked at all and were not tired. They knew this was the end of the day and they were going home.

"Are you ready, Red Mule?" Scrappie asked.

"I'm ready," he said. "The job is done. I had to wait, but I've got some money now to buy feed for my mules and food for myself."

"All right, Dick and Dinah," Scrappie called. "Let's go! Red Mule is ready."

The mules walked faster than their usual pace. They pulled the wagon onto the street and there was an awful noise as the disk clattered behind. Scrappie sat up on the springy seat, holding the lines. He looked hard at the truck drivers who drove too close to the team. If one got behind the wagon and blew his horn, Red Mule looked back, and the truck driver didn't blow his horn anymore.

"You know, Scrappie, I heard the mayor was going to stop me from chaining my disk harrow on behind the wagon and going down the street!" Red Mule shouted in Scrappie's ear. "He said my disk makes too much noise!"

"Who do you think reported us, Red Mule?" Scrappie asked.

"Oh, it's hard to tell!" Red Mule hollered. "Mayor Stewart says he's going to get a town ordinance to keep disk harrows off the street! This town has changed since I was a boy! I used to ride up and down these streets on my disk with a red-handled whip over my shoulder. I carried a whip for show but never used it. I had red tassels on my mules' bridles! It was a good ride back in them days on the old disk harrow behind Rock and Ruth! But this was before 1922, when they paved the streets in this town. That happened when I was seventeen. A lot of things have changed since then!"

Many cars pulled up behind the wagon and couldn't go around for the oncoming traffic. It was quitting time in Blakesburg for the shopkeepers and people who worked in the town. They were driving to their homes in the town and in the country. When the long line formed behind the mules and wagon, many of the drivers started blowing their horns. Red Mule looked back, but Scrappie couldn't look now. He had to look ahead and watch the traffic. Dick and Dinah didn't like to walk on the streets in the first place. They liked to step on dirt, where there was a little soft spring beneath their steel shoes. They didn't like to have trucks and automobiles get too close to them. The disk was making a loud noise on the concrete.

"Red Mule, I'll scoot over and let you have the mules now!" Scrappie said. "I'll soon be getting off!"

"Won't you go home with me, Scrappie?" Red Mule asked him.

This was the first time Red Mule had ever asked Scrappie to go home with him.

"Gee, Red Mule, I'd like to go home with you and Dick and Dinah," Scrappie said. "But I can't this afternoon. I'll have to ask Mom and Dad."

"Can you go home with me tomorrow night?" Red Mule asked as he slid over and took the lines from Scrappie.

"I'll ask them tonight and I'll let you know in the morning," Scrappie replied.

Red Mule drove up and stopped right in front of Scrappie's home so he could get off the wagon. At the same time, Scrappie's father drove up the street and turned left in front of the mules, who were holding up a long line of honking cars now. He drove into his driveway and stopped. He looked from the window of his car at the line of traffic, which looked like a funeral procession. Then he heard the loud clanking of the disk following the wagon as Red Mule drove on down the street and Scrappie came running across the yard.

"Scrappie, Scrappie!" Red Mule called back as he reined his mules to a stop. "I forgot to tell you! We'll plow the potato patch for Dave Bishop in the morning and you know. . . ."

"But the honking of the cars drowned out Red Mule's words. He and his mules had to move on while Scrappie and his father stood looking at the long line of creeping automobiles behind the team and wagon. As he went out of sight, big Red Mule was sitting up on the springboard seat, brave as a lion, holding the check lines in one of his big hands. He wasn't paying any attention to the cars behind him.

Scrappie Talks with His Father

"Well, if that's not a picture of progress, Scrappie!" Frank Lykins said to his son. "Look at that, won't you! Look at the automobiles that old plug team is holding back!"

"Dad, Dick and Dinah are not a plug mule team," Scrappie told his father. "Do you know what a plug team is? A plug team is one that's so old the mules can hardly walk, let alone pull a load. I've been driving Dick and Dinah today. They're young and powerful!"

"They don't look like it the way they're going up that street, holding up half the traffic in this town," his father said.

"But, Dad, Red Mule has to come this way to get out of town," Scrappie explained. "This is the only way he can go to the Sandy River bridge. Any other street would take him out of town on a different road. He has to cross the Sandy River to get home. He doesn't want to hold up traffic. He doesn't like being in traffic! He wants it to get past him and his mules!"

"Then he shouldn't be driving a team of mules," Frank Lykins told his son. "Our modern highways are made for automobiles, not mules. We have to have speed, for we have so many people. Mules are too slow and are out of place on modern highways!"

"Dad, mules have a gait and that's the way to let them walk," Scrappie answered. "Red Mule never lets his mules get out of their gait and they can work all day long."

"I'm glad to know that, Scrappie," Frank Lykins said, laying his hand on his son's tousled head. "I'll admit I know more about the grocery business than I do about mules. I've never ridden on the back of a mule, nor have I ever driven a team of mules in my life."

"You've missed a lot, Dad," Scrappie said, looking up and smiling at his father.

"Come along, Son, let's go in the house," his father said. "I want to talk to you."

Scrappie followed his father up the steps and into the living room. Then Frank Lykins pulled off his shoes and put his feet into his soft slippers.

"When you grow up and get older, Scrappie, you'll learn how wonderful it is to relax," his father said.

Scrappie watched him sit down in his big soft chair and put his feet up on a stool. His mother had left the Auckland Daily News on the arm of his chair. "When I come home from the store, I'm ready to drop," Mr. Lykins talked on, as he pulled a cigar from his inside coat pocket, lit it with a lighter, and puffed a cloud of smoke. "I like to be home with you and Mother. I like to sit here in my good soft chair and smoke and take it easy until supper is ready."

"Frank, you can't guess who we had for lunch today," Mrs. Lykins called. She came in from the kitchen, smiling. "I'll give you ten guesses."

"It couldn't have been Red Mule?"

"You guessed it, Dad!" Scrappie said happily.

"Oh, no!" his father said. "I was just teasing when I guessed it was Red Mule who had lunch with you! How could he ever get food inside his mouth with all that beard he's got? His face looks like a crow's nest made of red sticks!"

"Red Mule is a fine man," Scrappie said. "But he's hungry. I saw him eating feed from the mules' feedbox. I came on home for my lunch, but I couldn't eat for thinking about him. So Mom let me go back and bring him home to eat with me."

"Well, I hope this doesn't become a habit," his father said. "How do you feel about it, Mother? Do you want to cook for Red Mule?"

"Well, I can't say that I do, Frank," Mrs. Lykins

replied. "He will eat as much as a family of four."

"But Red Mule is hungry, Mom!" Scrappie interrupted her.

"Lucy Williams came by and told me she saw Red Mule throwing at something up in a tree and said she never heard such laughing as he was doing," Scrappie's mother said. "She said after she walked down the street and looked back, she saw you throwing, too."

"Mom, I saw Mrs. Williams on the other side of the street," Scrappie explained. "I knew how she'd talked about Red Mule. And she stopped there to find out something to run and tell you. She asked me what was the matter with Red Mule, why he was doing all that laughing."

"Tell us, Son, what did tickle Red Mule?" his father asked.

Scrappie told his father how Red Mule had found big clods of dirt in the lot Milford had plowed. "Red Mule said he knew then," Scrappie went on, "that the tractors weren't going to put his mules out of business and he was so happy he yelled and laughed. And he threw some of the clods up into the tree."

"Well, people are also talking about the way you work for Red Mule and never get paid, Scrappie," his father said. "When is Red Mule going to pay you?"

"Dad, Red Mule needs his money," Scrappie

said. "He's got to eat. He's got to feed Dick and Dinah!"

"Are you going to be another Red Mule?" Frank Lykins asked, looking seriously at his son. "A lot of people have asked me that. Everybody in this town knows how you tag around after Red Mule. They know how you sit up there on his wagon seat and drive his mules through town, with a load of plows, hoes, and feedboxes, and a disk harrow chained on behind! People laugh when they see you coming with a string of cars honking behind you. Son, that's not a picture of progress!"

"But, Dad, I like Dick and Dinah and the wagon better than a car," Scrappie said.

"Well, you probably won't when you're a year or two older! Now let me tell you something, Son, about Red Mule," Frank Lykins spoke seriously. "I remember the time when he was a respectable young man in this town. I was about your age then."

"Dad, isn't Red Mule still a respectable man?" Scrappie asked. "What is the matter with him?"

"Oh, yes, he's a law-abiding man and good in many ways," Scrappie's father explained, "but he's gone to seed. Do you know what people mean when they say something has 'gone to seed'?

"Not exactly," Scrappie replied.

"When something goes to seed, it's all

through," his father continued. "It hasn't any more value. That's the way people around here look at Red Mule. And mules are through, too. They're things of the past. They have no more usefulness. Old lazy mules have been Red Mule's downfall. I'll bet you don't even know his real name."

"Red Mule is his name to me," Scrappie said.

"That's the name all this young generation know him by," Frank Lykins said. "But his real name is Gabriel Gentry. That's a prettier name than Red Mule, isn't it?"

"Not to me!" Scrappie said. "That doesn't even sound like it ought to be his name. Red Mule is more like it."

"Scrappie, there was a time when Red Mule made money by plowing gardens in this town," his father said. "He lived in that little red-brick house on the river front where Donald Dunnaway lives now. He had a livery stable back on Second Street near the Mendall Blacksmith Shop. He lived with his mother. His father, Cy Gentry, died when Gabriel was younger than you are now. Gabriel made money in those days. He wore fine clothes and he drove the best-looking horses, with red tassels on their bridles, brass knobs on their hames, and little bells that jingled on their polished harnesses. But that was the horse-and-buggy days. Since then we've had the automobile and the air age. Gabriel is still living in the horse-and-buggy days. He's fooled around with mules too long.

Now, do you want to grow up and be a man like him?"

"Yes, Dad, I'd like to be like Red Mule," Scrappie answered quietly. "I don't think I want to work in a grocery store."

"There are plenty of ways to make a living besides driving mules or running a grocery," his father said. "You'll probably have a dozen ideas before you decide. Red Mule lives somewhere out of Blakesburg, doesn't he? No one seems to know exactly where he does live."

"Dad, he's asked me to go home with him tomorrow night," Scrappie said. "That's what I want to ask you."

Frank Lykins looked at his son.

"Yes," he said slowly, "you can go. I want you to find out whether you really want to be a mule driver!"

"Frank, do you think that's all right?" Scrappie's mother asked as she came from the kitchen, where she was preparing supper. "Are you sure of what you are doing?"

"Oh, yes, Mother," he said, "I'm quite sure. One of these days Scrappie will be a young man and he'll be wearing a nice suit of clothes and will have a pretty girl holding onto his arm. There won't be any more Red Mule and mule teams then! Let him go now and enjoy himself! Let him be a real boy!"

"Gee, Dad, that's wonderful!" Scrappie

shouted as he jumped up from his chair and put his arms around his father's neck. "You've made me very happy!"

"But, Frank," Mary Lykins argued, "where does Red Mule live? Do you know, Scrappie?"

"No, I don't, Mom," he replied. "But if you'll let me go, I'll tell you after tomorrow night."

"But, Scrappie, I'll worry about you," she said. "I'll be wondering about what kind of a bed you'll be sleeping in and what you'll have to eat. I just can't imagine Red Mule cooking anything you can eat!"

"Now, Mother, quit worrying and let Scrappie and me handle this," Frank Lykins said with a wink. "Red Mule's like a boy when it comes to animals. Let Scrappie go with him. Let Scrappie worry about something to eat and a bed to sleep in. He won't starve overnight!"

"Dad, I'll always love you for this," Scrappie said as he took his arms from around his father's neck. "I'll never be able to go to sleep tonight for thinking about going home with Red Mule to-morrow night!"

Frank Lykins chuckled and rumpled Scrappie's hair. "It will be a real experience for you, Son. I'll be interested to hear all about your visit when you get home." "So will I, Scrappie," Mrs. Lykins said, with a smile.

Scrappie Goes Home with the Mules

"It's hard to believe I'm going home with you," Scrappie said to Red Mule after they finished work the next day, and hitched up Dick and Dinah.

"I've wanted to explain something to you for quite a while, Scrappie," Red Mule said, as they climbed into the wagon seat and he started the mules. "You must have thought it's strange that I've been sharing the work with you but not the money for the work."

"That's all right, Red Mule. I don't care about money."

"It's not reasonable not to care about money, but I think you'll understand after you visit me tonight. I've had something in my mind for a long time. You're in for a big surprise tonight,

Scrappie!"

"Gee, that's wonderful, Red Mule!" Scrappie said excitedly. "I can hardly wait to know what it is! I know it will be good! I've always known that you are fair and honest about anything you do. I've never worried about your not paying me. I've enjoyed working with you."

As they continued down Main Street, the cars whizzed past them.

"Hiya, Red Mule!" Bouncer Williams yelled from the sidewalk as they passed. "Hiya, Little Mule!"

Then he ran away, laughing. Scrappie watched Bouncer from the corner of his eye as he ran around behind the courthouse. He laughed and pointed to Scrappie and Red Mule as he ran.

"I'll make him laugh one of these days," Scrappie told Red Mule. "He's been getting smart with me because I work with you. I've let it pass because his mother is my Mom's friend, but I'm getting tired of it."

"Pay no attention to him," Red Mule said. "There are a lot of people like him. They don't have any fun in life and don't want anybody else to have any fun either."

"I know Bouncer," Scrappie said. "I have to go to school with him. He pokes fun at you and me."

"Now, Scrappie, never worry about that," Red

Mule said. "There are bigger things in this world to think about. The surprise I'm going to show you tonight is one."

When they left Blakesburg they drove across a bridge over the Sandy River. It was a narrow bridge, built seventy-five years before in the horse-and-buggy days. Cars had to wait on each end now when a horse or mule team went over, to keep from spooking the animals. The teams that crossed in one day could be counted on the fingers on one hand and there would be fingers left, but when a team went over, it took a few minutes and the cars had to line up on each end and wait. But Red Mule and Scrappie had to cross the river with Dick and Dinah, and the cars had to wait.

When they reached U.S. 23, the cars zoomed past them like big bullets on singing wheels.

"Scrappie, I remenber when this was a plain old dirt road," Red Mule sighed wistfully. "It was a pretty road, with a lot of curves in it. The dirt was soft on the mules' feet. I've come over this road in April many times before with my wagon loaded. Those old apple trees up there are about all that's still the way it used to be here. They're white with blooms again this year. They've been white with blossoms every year since I can remember. I remember another world here, Scrappie, a wonderful world of powerful mule and horse teams, rubber-tired buggies, fringed sur-

reys, express wagons, and jolt wagons. I wish you could have known that world, Scrappie!"

"I wish I could have, too," Scrappie said.

"But mules do hold up traffic," Scrappie thought. "They are slow, like Dad said. This is a faster age." Scrappie was thinking of the Sandy River bridge they had just crossed and how they had held up traffic. He didn't tell Red Mule his thoughts.

They reached Colton's Branch and turned to their left.

"See, we've even got a hard road up this creek!" Red Mule exclaimed. "Got it four years ago. Not many soft dirt roads are left for the mules and horses. But we'll soon be on one!"

"Get up, Dick and Dinah!" Scrappie said happily.

"Turn right here and we'll get on a good mule road."

Scrappie reined Dick and Dinah onto a narrow road between two high hills.

"Watch 'em step on this soft road, won't you?" Red Mule shouted above the noise of the creaking wagon. "They like it!"

Scrappie looked up to his right, then over to his left, at the high, wooded hills, where the trees were beginning to leaf out. Alongside this winding little dirt road was a stream that murmured over the rocks as it ran toward the river and the sea.

"Gee, this is pretty country, Red Mule," Scrappie said softly. "I wish we lived out here. How did you ever find such a wonderful place?"

"You know I used to live in Blakesburg," Red Mule said, "but it got so that with all this modern living after the cars came, mules and barns were no longer welcome in town. So I left with them, Scrappie. I bought land here and moved to the right fork of Colton's Branch."

They drove on up the little road and the farther they went, the faster Dick and Dinah walked.

"This is the first time I ever saw 'em get out of their gait, Red Mule!" Scrappie said.

They're getting close to home," the big man replied. "A mule likes his home. He likes a certain hole of water to drink from, a certain manger and box to eat from, and a certain place to sleep."

Then they reached another place, where two little streams came from two valleys to make the stream and valley they had followed.

"Turn right, Scrappie," Red Mule told him.

The road was very narrow now and the hills were much higher. In a few minutes Scrappie looked up and saw a big barn that looked as if it was ready to fall down. The road he was following led into the barn entry. Here the mules stopped.

The Big Surprise

"Well, here's the place," Red Mule said.

"But where's the house, Red Mule?" Scrappie asked.

"Up there in the hay," the big man answered. "Dick and Dinah have their stalls down here."

"Gee, this is wonderful!" Scrappie said excitedly. "I'd like this kind of life!"

He wondered how Red Mule cooked up there in the hay, but he didn't ask him.

Scrappie helped Red Mule unhitch Dick and Dinah and take their harness off, then Red Mule turned the mules loose in the barn lot so they could wallow in the dry dust, then get water from the stream that flowed across the lot. Next, he put feed in their boxes and showed Scrappie how to throw hay down from the hayloft into their mangers below. Red Mule had him fork more hay down into the long manger in the big section where there weren't any mule stalls.

"What's all this hay for?" Scrappie shouted down at Red Mule.

"You just wait and see!" he called back.

As Scrappie came down the ladder from the hayloft, he watched Red Mule walk through the barn entry and to the upper end of the barn lot, where he opened a big, swinging gate. He began calling: "Come, boys! Come, girls! Come, boys! Come on, girls! Come on, boys!"

Suddenly, Scrappie heard the pounding of hoofs! The sound was like thunder in the distance. As the sound of thunder got closer, Scrappie's heart started beating faster, and he started running to a far corner in the barn lot. When he looked up the hollow he saw the mules coming—dozens of them. When he saw this herd of galloping mules with their heads thrust forward, their ears laid back, and their tails riding on the wind, Scrappie ran for the fence. He climbed up on it and started counting. But he lost count when some of the mules jumped in front of others. His heart was really pounding now. He'd never seen anything as pretty in his life as this herd of young, high-spirited mules. They galloped into the big stall, which took up nearly all of the barn.

"What do you think of 'em?" Red Mule asked as he came walking down after the last mule had leaped through the big barn door.

"I didn't know you had any more mules!" Scrappie said with excitement. "They're the prettiest things I've ever seen!"

"I've got thirty-five mules here, and Dick and Dinah make thirty-seven," he told Scrappie.

"But we can't work all these mules," Scrappie said. "What are you going to do with them?"

"I'm going to save 'em," Red Mule replied.

"Save 'em from what?" Scrappie asked.

Red Mule didn't answer him. He started climbing up the ladder again to the hayloft.

"Scrappie, how would you like to own a mule?" Red Mule asked as he stopped on the ladder and looked down at Scrappie, who was coming up behind him. "Do you think you'd like to own one?"

"Sure I would!" he replied quickly. "If I owned as many mules as you I'd feel like I was the richest boy in the world!"

"Well," Red Mule said as he started on up, "let's eat our supper and then we'll do some talking."

He led Scrappie down an open passage in the hay-filled loft to an open corner. Scrappie saw a big tin box and some wooden packing crates. Red Mule opened the tin box and got out a box of crackers, a block of cheese, and a box of brown sugar.

"This is our supper," he told Scrappie, as he motioned for him to sit down on one of the wooden crates. "Now in the morning, we won't have breakfast here. I'll have a cup of coffee at the Dinner Bell, and I'll let you go home for your breakfast."

"That will be all right, Red Mule," Scrappie said as he hungrily eyed the cheese, crackers, and brown sugar.

Red Mule sliced the cheese with his pocket-knife and they ate cheese and brown sugar on crackers. Scrappie had never had a meal like this before. He thought he had never eaten food that tasted better. He ate heartily as Red Mule gave him food first, then helped himself.

"Scrappie, I'm a little older than your father," Red Mule told him. "I lived with my mother as a young man, but when she died many years ago, I lived with my mules. I've lived with them ever since."

"Gee, I'd like this kind of life," Scrappie said. "How did you ever find such a good way to live?"

"Scrappie, I found it by circumstance," Red Mule said as he laid a big cracker loaded with brown sugar on his tongue. "Trucks came first and replaced the jolt wagons and teams. Then we got better roads and the trucks could go faster. Then we got more and bigger trucks. It just about took all the haulin' away from the mule teams

and jolt wagons. We could still use mules for a lot of things, like plowing ground and snaking saw logs from the timber woods. But then we got the tractors with plows and even got tractors to haul logs from the woods. The mules didn't have any work left for them. Then people started buying them up and hauling 'em away to be butchered for fertilizer and dog food. Did you ever hear of anything like it?"

"No, I never did," Scrappie said. He was shocked. "But I do see big truckloads of mules and horses going through Blakesburg."

"They're going to the cannery," Red Mule said. "When I see a truckload of 'em, I turn my head and cry. I really cry, Scrappie. There's no more work for these good mules and they have to die. It breaks my heart, Scrappie."

Tears welled up in Red Mule's big blue eyes.

He sliced more cheese for Scrappie and himself.

"Scrappie, I couldn't have saved all the mules down there if it hadn't been for you," Red Mule told him.

"How have I helped you, Red Mule?" Scrappie asked, looking up at him with surprise.

"Well, you've worked for me off and on for almost two years and I've not paid you," Red Mule said. "I've taken the money I should have paid to you and bought more mules!"

"Gee, what's wrong with that?" Scrappie asked. "I'm happy about it. I'm glad I'm helping you save these mules. We're saving 'em together, Red Mule! It makes me happy to know that we are!"

"Well, I'm an honest man, Scrappie," Red Mule said softly. "People don't work for nothing, and I don't expect anybody to work for me for nothing. I've had something in mind I want to do for you for a long time."

Scrappie stopped eating and looked straight at Red Mule.

"I'll tell you the real big surprise I have for you," Red Mule said as he held a cracker loaded with brown sugar in his hand. "It wasn't the number of mules I showed you a few minutes ago. Scrappie, I need a partner. I want to make you a junior partner to go into the mule business with me. I want to give you a third of everything!"

"You don't mean that, Red Mule?" Scrappie asked.

"Yes, I do, Scrappie," he replied softly, looking at the small boy on the crate beside him. "I mean just what I said. You and I can save a lot of mules together. What do you think about it?"

"I want to be your junior partner, Red Mule!" Scrappie replied. "I know we can work together and save the mules. I'll do all I can to help feed them now! Does it cost a lot of money to feed 'em?"

"All I can make and more, too," the big man said. "If I had the money to buy 'em, cheap as they are, and enough land to pasture 'em, I'd own a thousand mules. I'd save that many. It ain't the mules' fault that all this has happened, Scrappie! Mules are as good to work now as they ever were. They've just lost out. Times have changed. This is another age."

"I hate to hear that," Scrappie said.

"In a hundred years from now boys like you will be askin' what a mule used to look like," Red Mule told him. "I used to have money in the bank. I had nearly enough to keep me the rest of my life. But I bought this barn, a hundred acres of land, and all these mules. I don't have enough land now to pasture my mules, and that's why I have to feed 'em hay."

"I'll be thinking about feedin' 'em," Scrappie said as his eyes grew heavy with sleep.

That night Red Mule and Scrappie slept on the hay with quilts over them. Scrappie woke when the rooster crowed for midnight. He looked up through the cracks in the barn at the stars in the blue April sky. Down under him he heard the loud breathing of the mules. Now and then two mules would quarrel and one would squeal and bite the other. Once in the night he heard Red Mule rise up from his bed of hay and yell, "Cut it out down there!"

Scrappie's Father Makes a Decision

Next morning when Red Mule stopped at the Dinner Bell for coffee, Scrappie hurried up the street to his home for breakfast.

He brushed the hay from his clothes carefully before he tried to open the door. It was locked. Then he knocked on the door.

"Just a minute!", Scrappie heard his father call. "Take it easy! Just a minute!"

When the door opened, Mr. Lykins stood there in his pajamas, robe, and house slippers.

"Oh, so it's you, Scrappie!" he exclaimed happily. "Mother! Oh, Mother, come and look! Scrappie is here! Come and look where he slept last night!"

Mr. Lykins stood in the doorway until Scrappie's mother came.

"Darling, look at our Scrappie," he said when

she got to the door. Then he laughed loudly, and said, "I told you to let Scrappie go home with Red Mule!"

Scrappie's mother and father stood looking at him and shaking with laughter.

"Tell me what's so funny and I'll laugh too," Scrappie told them.

"It's the hay in your hair, Scrappie," his mother said, laughing louder. "You've not washed your face or combed your hair!"

Scrappie's hand went up to his head. He felt hay in his hair, all right.

"I thought I got it all," he said, turning to walk back down the steps to brush himself off again.

"Sure, Dad, I slept in the hay," Scrappie admitted. "I never slept better in my life!"

"Come to breakfast, Scrappie, and tell us all about your visit with Red Mule," his mother said.

"I've got something wonderful to tell you!" Scrappie said.

His parents went back into the house, and Scrappie got all the hay out of his hair that he could. Then he went inside the house. "I wonder if Red Mule washed this morning," Scrappie thought. "I wonder if he combed his hair. He might have washed his face and combed his hair when he first got up this morning. He could have washed in the creek that flows through his barn lot. But if he washed his face and combed his long hair and beard, he did it before I got up."

"Sit down, Son, and join us," his father said when Scrappie went into the breakfast room. "We want to know about your visit."

"Yes, tell us about it, Scrappie," his mother joined in. "Where does Red Mule live?"

"Mom, he lives way out of town in a big barn that looks like it's ready to fall down," Scrappie said. "But it's a swell place! Gee, I liked it out there! And something great has happened! Let me tell you . . ."

"Where is Red Mule's place?" his father interrupted him.

"Up Colton's Branch, then up the right fork of Colton's Branch, and then up the right fork of the right fork," Scrappie told them.

"You remember well, Scrappie," his father said. "I could follow those directions."

"Did you sleep with anything over you?" his mother asked.

"Oh, yes, a quilt," Scrappie said. "Red Mule and I slept in the loft above the mule stalls. We slept on the soft hay under quilts."

"It was cool last night for April," his father said. "I had to set the furnace up ten degrees!"

"Red Mule said it's dogwood winter," Scrappie explained. "But he says dogwood winter will help him. He says the trees leaf more in a dark, cool time and his mules in that hundred-acre pasture need green leaves to eat!"

"How many mules has he got?" his father asked.

"You mean, how many mules have we got?" Scrappie corrected him. "We have thirty-five out there on the pasture and Dick and Dinah, that we work. I'm Red Mule's partner! I own a third of thirty-seven mules! Think of it, Mom! Think of it, Dad! I am rich in mules!"

Scrappie's father was silent. He looked across the table quickly at his wife and she looked at him. A worried look came over Frank Lykins' face, like a dark cloud that spreads over a blue sky before a storm.

"Scrappie, you mean to say that Red Mule gave you an interest in his mules?" his mother asked him. "You mean he just gave you a third interest in all those mules?"

"It's not exactly that way, Mom," Scrappie explained as he ate hot oatmeal and drank his glass of milk. "It's like this. I've worked for Red Mule after school and Saturdays for almost two years. He's never paid me. Well, Red Mule took some of the money he should have paid me to buy mules. That's how he has been able to save thirty-seven mules. And this is all right with me. I'm glad he did that and saved the mules. I always told you Red Mule was a good man. He's an honest man, too. He wanted to pay me so he gave me one-third interest. Think of it!"

"That's just what I'm doing, Scrappie," Frank Lykins spoke seriously. "Do you realize what it takes to feed thirty-seven mules? Do you know that you will be responsible for one-third of the feed it takes to feed these mules? You could give your one-third interest back to Red Mule and come out ahead financially!"

"You don't think I did the right thing?" Scrappie asked as he held the spoonful of oatmeal before his mouth. "You want me to give my part of the mules back to Red Mule?"

"No, no, Son, I won't say that," his father said. "I'll say this—you are very young to take on that much responsibility and have to worry about feeding all those mules. You're taking a great chance!"

"But we are feeding the mules," Scrappie said. "We're plowing lots and truck patches and hauling a few things and buying feed for the mules and food for Red Mule."

Scrappie put the oatmeal in his mouth and ate slowly. His eyes started welling up with tears.

"Frank, remember that when you started a little grocery store in this town, you took a chance too," Mary Lykins reminded her husband. "You made a lot of mistakes in your business, too, but you learned by making them. Yes, Scrappie is taking a chance, but I think we ought to be for his doing it! Look what he has earned, Frank! Scrappie owns one-third of thirty-seven mules! Tell me another boy in this town who has worked like Scrappie and who has as much to show for his work!"

"Say, Mary, you do have a point," Frank Lykins said, looking up and smiling at his wife. "Scrappie has accomplished more than any other boy in this town. He's worked with Red Mule on the side, and has never missed a day of school. He's been an honor student for two years. I think we should help Scrappie work out some easier way to feed his mules!"

"Gee, Dad, that makes me feel good," Scrappie said. Then a big smile came over his face as he dried the tears with the back of his hand.

"Son, give me time to do some thinking about it. Right now I've got to hurry to the store!"

"And I have to hurry, too," Scrappie said. "Red Mule and I are going to work for Tobias Reffitt today. Red Mule is already there! My partner needs me!"

That evening when Scrappie came into the living room after supper, his father was sitting in his easy chair.

"Scrappie, I've been thinking about what you told me this morning and I've got an idea," his father said. "Sit down and I'll tell you what I have in mind."

Scrappie sat down in a chair opposite his father.

"You know, Son, I've been thinking about you a lot today," Mr. Lykins said softly. "You are now in business. You own mules. When you own something, you're responsible for its welfare. You are as responsible for feeding those mules as Red Mule is."

"I know I am, Dad," Scrappie said as he watched his father blow a wisp of smoke toward the ceiling. "That's the reason Red Mule and I worked late today. We've got more jobs to do.

We got a job to go over a lot Milford Royster had plowed and disked for Ike Abrams. He didn't plow close enough to the fence, and he left big clods. So we did that lot after we'd plowed and disked Tobias Reffitt's garden. Dad, I know we've got thiry-seven mules to feed!"

"Scrappie, you're going to learn a lot about property and responsibility," his father told him. "Now, you never cared much for the grocery store. Well, I started out with my little store after your mother and I were married. I had a time getting along and making it pay at first. Now I own my store building on Main Street. I don't have to rent it any longer. I own this home we live in. And I own three farms. But I've had to work for all of this. It looks like I've managed pretty well, doesn't it?"

"It sure does, Dad," Scrappie replied. "But, Dad, I never had anything against the grocery store. I just like to work with mules better than in a store."

"The grocery business I have built with my own head and hands has done well for us," Mr. Lykins said. "It has bought land enough to pasture your thirty-seven mules and more. I could rent that pasture to somebody for seventy-five dollars a month. I'm willing to rent this pasture to you and Red Mule for your mules!"

"Gee, Dad, that's wonderful," Scrappie said.

"But how much will you charge us for thirty-seven mules? Red Mule and I can't pay you seventy-five dollars a month."

"It will take some planning," his father said. "How about you working for me in the store part of the time? Say you work for me by the hour. I've been thinking about fifty cents an hour."

"But I've got to be with Red Mule on some jobs that are coming up," Scrappie said.

"I know, but you won't be working with Red Mule all the time," his father said. "School will soon be out for the summer and you'll have spare time. And besides, I have a lot of things shipped to me regularly by freight that you and Red Mule can haul from the railway station. I'll quit hiring Milford Royster to haul them by truck!"

"It's a bargain, Dad!" Scrappie said happily. "Red Mule and I will haul your freight from the railway station with our mules and I'll work for you after school!"

"Then my pasture is ready for thirty-seven mules," his father said. "Your word is good enough for me. You and Red Mule can take them there any time. The grass is ready for them. This will keep you from having a big feed bill."

"Gee, that's great, Dad!" Scrappie said. "There's no one like my Dad when it comes to solving a problem!"

Mules Triumph over Tractors

Before the apple trees had shed their blossoms in the back yards of the homes in Blakesburg, Red Mule and Scrappie had moved their mules to his father's pasture. They did this during spring vacation. Soon the vacation was over and Scrappie was back in school.

Each day when school was out, Scrappie carried his books into his father's grocery and started work. Some days he filled orders, getting each item down from the shelf as Miss Tyler, the bookkeeper, called it out to him. "One large can of tomatoes," she would say, "one can of corn, cream style, a five-pound sack of sugar." He would put the groceries in a carton and get the order ready for the delivery boy. On other days, Scrappie would unpack cases and stack the cans in neat pyramids. He often made deliveries when a customer was in a hurry and couldn't wait for the regular delivery.

There were plenty of things that needed to be done all the time in a grocery store. Scrappie was surprised to find himself getting interested in the business. When salesmen came in with new products, Scrappie's father would call him over and ask his opinion. Sometimes they would decide to buy and sometimes Mr. Lykins just knew the product wasn't the kind of thing his customers would want. Scrappie saw that everyone in town had a great deal of respect for his father's opinion and would ask his advice on all kinds of things having nothing to do with groceries. "Dad, I bet you answer more questions than the mayor does," Scrappie would say, and his father would laugh.

One Saturday afternoon after a particularly busy time, Mr. Lykins said, "Scrappie, you've put in a long, hard day. Why don't you go on home?"

But Scrappie wasn't ready to go. "I'll wait and help Red Mule with the freight load he's bringing in," he said. "Dick and Dinah will be disappointed if I don't give them apples after they finish hauling our load."

In a few minutes, Dick and Dinah came down the street. Red Mule and Scrappie carried the boxes into the store and Miss Tyler checked the delivery. After they had stacked the last one, and Dick and Dinah were chewing a final apple, Red

Mule and Scrappie saw Mace McDowell drive up to the curb on the other side of the street, where he parked his horse-and-mule truck. It was loaded with mules. They were packed into the truck like sardines in a can. Each mule tried to get his eyes up level with a crack in the slats on the sides so he could look out. Mace got out of the cab and went into the Dinner Bell. As Dick and Dinah pulled the wagon away from the store, one of the mules in the truck looked across the street and saw them. Then he brayed, and Dick and Dinah stopped pulling the jolt wagon. Dinah brayed back to him.

"Listen to that, won't you, Scrappie!" Red Mule said. "It breaks my heart to hear that pitiful mule talk! That's old Mace! He's stopped at the Dinner Bell to get himself some coffee. He'll be driving to Columbus tonight. He's taking that load to the cannery!"

"Can't Mace make a living some other way?" Scrappie asked Red Mule.

"I've asked him that many times," the big man said, with tears welling up in his eyes. "Think of just going around and buying up mules and trucking big loads like that one to the cannery! I can count twelve on that truck, Scrappie! Think of twelve mules being taken away from the little farms to be killed!"

Then another mule brayed from the truck, and old Dick answered him.

"That's a Lost Creek mule," Red Mule told Scrappie. "He brays just a little different from the Tiger River or the Sandy River mules. Mules speak a different language on Lost Creek."

"Red Mule, you understand mule language better than I do," Scrappie said.

"I'm older than you," the big man said. "You know what that mule said to old Dick? He said, 'You're lucky.' And old Dick answered him, 'You bet we are! We've got good masters.' That's you and me, Scrappie!" Another mule brayed from the truck, and Dinah replied in a long, mournful tone.

"Where was he from and what did he say, Red Mule?"

"He's a Tiger River mule and he said to Dinah, 'We don't know where we're going. We don't believe we're going to farms. We might be going to the cannery!' And old Dinah replied, 'Kick the slats off the truck! Jump into the street! Then run back to the green pastures! Escape before it's too late!'"

"Gee, Red Mule, you sure can understand mules," Scrappie said.

"Just sit there and listen! They'll all get to braying so loud here in a minute that Mace will have to leave his coffee and jump into his truck and drive it out of Blakesburg! He's not supposed to park it there, anyway. But I'm glad he has! It lets other people hear the sad talk of those departing mules! They don't want to leave here!"

Red Mule was right. All the mules in the truck started to bray at once, and Dick and Dinah answered. Mrs. Ezra Williams came down the street and stopped and put her hands over her ears. She looked toward Red Mule, Scrappie, Dick, and Dinah and then looked at the truckload of braying mules parked on Main Street. She went toward the mayor's office in a hurry with her hands over her ears.

"She's going to report that to the mayor!" Red Mule shouted in Scrappie's ear. "Mace had better get away from the Dinner Bell while he can! His mules are making too much noise! The mayor won't have that in Blakesburg! It's too bad he can't understand mule talk. If he could understand the things they are saying he'd have Mace locked up in jail!"

Scrappie and Red Mule had to put their hands over their ears to drown the braying of the twelve mules who were calling to Dick and Dinah. Mace came out of the Dinner Bell just as the mayor walked up the street. He jumped into his truck and drove down Main Street while his mules put their noses against the high truck bed and brayed.

Scrappie and Red Mule still got jobs, but sometimes Scrappie was worried. The next Saturday morning as he lay awake in bed, he wondered if his father hadn't been right all the time about the mules. "Even if Red Mule and I love mules, they are still behind the times," he thought. "Looking back to old times the way Red Mule does isn't enough. We've got to find something that mules can do better than machinery can."

This was the day that Red Mule and Scrappie shared an order with the three tractor owners to haul twenty cords of driftwood to the Greenwood County Jail. Although he wouldn't admit it to anyone, Scrappie didn't think the mules had much of a chance. Today the people of Blakesburg would see how much more wood the tractors could haul than the mules could. If he and Red Mule got their full share, they would get five of the twenty cords to haul. That would be five good loads up the Sandy River bank. But there would be Milford Royster, Jad Warnock, and Sylvester Lybrooks—all with their fast tractors. It would be a race, and how much chance did Scrappie and Red Mule have? Red Mule wasn't worried. He thought they would do all right. He was going to use a young, powerful span of big mules, Sorrel Giant and Queen Lucy, to compete. He'd let Dick and Dinah rest on this day.

The Sandy River had flooded during the winter and left piles of driftwood that the March and

April suns had seasoned. Years before, Red Mule had started hauling driftwood to the people of Blakesburg to burn in fireplaces and stoves and to use for kindling. Hauling spring driftwood had been a profitable business for him until Milford Royster, Jad Warnock, and Sylvester Lybrooks bought their tractors and started competing with him. Now they were sharing this business. Adam Linwood, Greenwood County jailer, gave the order each year to all four. The one who hauled the most on that day got the most pay. So each tried to haul as much as he could.

This Saturday the tractor drivers began competing among themselves and overlooking Red Mule and Scrappie until suddenly something happened. Milford got too close to Sandy River, and his tractor wheels started spinning and then sank down into the mud. Jad tried to pull him out and his tractor stuck, too. Then Sylvester tried to pull Jad's tractor out, and he bogged down.

"Now we'll get the business," Red Mule told Scrappie while a crowd gathered on the river bank and looked on and cheered for the mules. "Let 'em set there in the mud! It's not neighborly, but trucks and tractors have never been good neighbors to mules!"

Red Mule and Scrappie laid the driftwood on their jolt wagon. They let the mules stay in their gait up the river bank to the jailhouse, but when they came back empty, they let them run all the way. They took load after load up the bank and raced back, thinking each time that their competition would have the tractors out when they returned. But they didn't. Milford went up into Blakesburg and got Dave Attlebury to bring his big truck. Dave hooked a chain onto Milford's tractor, but the truck wheels were soon buried in the sand, too.

"Scrappie, they'll come to us this time!" Red Mule said, as they kept hauling.

Milford, Jay, and Sylvester worked most of the day trying to get their tractors and Dave Attlebury's truck out of the mud. And all day Red Mule and Scrappie hauled driftwood. That evening, they let Sorrel Giant and Queen Lucy walk down the riverbank to get the last load.

"Say, Red Mule," Milford said, walking over. "We're stuck! We're really stuck!"

"I see you are," Red Mule said, grinning.

"Do you suppose your mules could pull these tractors out?"

"Yes, but my mules are a little tired," Red Mule said. "We've had to put in three-fourths of that big order at the jail today. Sorrel Giant could pull one of the tractors out at a time if the singletree didn't break. Any mule I've got will pull in water up to his belly. His engine won't choke out! He won't bog down!"

Milford looked down and shoved gravel around with his shoe.

"How much would you charge to pull our tractors and the truck out?" he asked, looking up quickly at Red Mule.

"It will be high," Red Mule said. "We'll have to charge you by the foot, won't we, Scrappie? Two bucks a foot will be about right, don't you think, Scrappie?"

"Two dollars a foot?" Milford said, his face getting red.

"That's the least we'll take," Scrappie replied. "We've got pasture for our mules now. We've got hay in the barn to feed 'em this winter, and we've got money to buy more mules!"

"I won't pay that," Milford said.

"You'll have to have mules for that job," Red Mule told him. "There've been heavy rains up the river and the water is rising, too. No gasoline-powered vehicle can pull you out of there! Only the sure-footed, reliable mules can do it, and we've got all the mules left around here! It's all right with us if you want to stay stuck, ain't it, Scrappie?"

He clucked to the mules, and Sorrel Giant and Queen Lucy walked on to get the last load. Scrappie and Red Mule loaded the wood and were starting back when Milford came running over.

"We'll pay you that, Red Mule!" he said. "I've talked to the boys. We've agreed!

The water is rising fast! Unhitch from your wagon and bring the mules! Maybe you can save us!"

"Our Sorrel Giant and Queen Lucy will save your tractors," Red Mule said. "We'll be over as soon as we can unhitch and get the drag chains from around the rough lock and the binding pole."

"Two dollars a foot!" Scrappie said. "We have to pull each tractor and the truck more than fifty feet! That's over two hundred feet and we will make over four hundred dollars, Red Mule! Gee, that's money! That will save six, seven, or eight, maybe nine, more mules! They're dirt cheap now! Not anybody wants to buy a mule but us!"

More people in Blakesburg had heard about the tractors and truck being stuck in the soft sand at the river's edge. They knew it was rising now at a foot an hour. Many Blakesburg people came down to see if the river would get the truck and tractors. Scrappie's father was in the crowd gathered on the river bank. Mrs. Ezra Williams and her son, Bouncer, were in the crowd, too.

When Red Mule backed the span of big mules into the river, Scrappie waded in and fastened the drag chain to the first tractor. Red Mule had to hold back with all his might on the lines. Then Scrappie told him to let them go. The giant mules bent low as they heaved forward with a great surge of power. They pulled the tractor slowly up the dry riverbank. There was a great applause for the mules when they did this.

"Our mules are showing them something, ain't

they, Scrappie?" Red Mule whispered, when Scrappie unhooked the chain and came back to him. "Now let's get the other two tractors and the truck!"

When they brought the second tractor out, a great shout went up. And when they pulled the third tractor out, the mules got a greater applause. Then came the real test of the mules' strength. The last job was the two-ton truck, and water was up in the engine now. Red Mule backed the mules up to the truck, and Scrappie fastened the chain. Dave Attlebury shifted his truck out of gear and sat at the steering wheel to guide it. The big mules got down and really pulled, an inch at a time, until they pulled it from the muck. This was the greatest display of mule strength the people in Blakesburg had ever seen. A great applause— clapping of hands, whistles, and shouts—went up!

After Red Mule had stepped off the distances, three feet for each step, Jad Warnock, Sylvester Lybrooks, Milford Royster, and Dave Attlebury walked up and paid him in cash. For every step he had taken when he measured the distances his mules had pulled the tractors and truck, he got six dollars, two dollars for each foot. They paid Red Mule in greenbacks. Scrappie had never seen Red Mule stuff so much money into his pockets before. The people on the river bank watched this, too. This was one time they had seen mules triumph over trucks and tractors!

Scrappie Finds a Way

Red Mule felt rich. "I knew we'd show them! Those tractors would be stuck in the mud yet if it wasn't for our mules! That was a fine sight, Scrappie, after all the bragging those fellows did, to see them sitting there helpless, having to beg us to pull them out of the mud!"

Scrappie laughed. "Our mules did the job and none of the tractors could. We sure won!" But then he thought, "Yes, we won, but only for a day. The mules have to eat every day. What are we going to do now? Plowing gardens and truck patches is over. All the work we have for our mules is to haul a few things from the railway station for Dad. Dad was right about mules. He knows what progress means. Milford Royster is pulling logs from the timber woods with his tractor. Jad Warnock is hauling gravel and sand from the river with his tractor. Sylvester Lybrooks is pulling a big cultivator with his tractor in the Sandy River bottoms. Red Mule and I don't have any more jobs to do with our mules. We will soon have to go cut hay and store it to feed them this winter. Just as Dad said, tractors don't eat anything when they're not working."

Scrappie walked into the living room, where his father was sitting with his feet propped up, his paper on his lap. He was asleep. Scrappie tiptoed over so he wouldn't wake him. He picked the paper up gently and sat down across from his father to read the sports page. As he started turning to the sports page, he suddenly saw a little headline: TURKEY IS USING OUR MULES. Then he forgot about the sports page.

Scrappie read in this small news item that the U.S. Government had purchased several hundred mules to send to parts of the world where it would be difficult to use mechanized equipment. Scrappie was so elated over finding this story in the paper that he cut it out with his Mom's scissors and put the clipping in his pocket. "But the paper doesn't say who in our Government is sending the mules to Turkey," he thought. Then he took the clipping from his pocket and read it again. It definitely didn't say who was sending the mules.

"Maybe mules are on their way back,"

Scrappie thought. "If some use could only be found for mules, then our problem would be solved. Dad is right. We can't go on feeding our mules year after year and not have anything for them to do. But if we can only find a use for them, Red Mule will be sleeping in a feather bed and he'll have an account at the bank like he had when he was a young man. I can show Bouncer something. Then he won't be going around and saying that I smell like a mule and that he has to hold his nose every time he passes me."

Scrappie kept thinking about what he'd seen in the paper about the mules when he went upstairs to his room and went to bed. He couldn't go to sleep for thinking about finding places where mules could still be used. When he went to sleep he was still thinking about it. He knew he had to write to somebody in the United States Government to find out.

Next morning when Scrappie was awakened by his mother's tapping the ceiling below his bed with a broom handle, he had the answer. He knew what he was going to do. He was going to sit down after breakfast and write a letter to the President of the United States. If anybody knew a place that needed mules, he should be the one.

Here is the letter Scrappie sent:

Blakesburg, Ky.

Dwight D. Eisenhower
President of the United States
White House Washington, D.C.

Dear Mister President:

We've got a problem down here and I thought
you might be able to help us. I have a good friend
and a partner in business by the name of Red
Mule. Red Mule and I like mules and we try to
save them from the canneries. There isn't enough
work for mules here now that people are using
tractors.

My name is Frank Lykins, but people call me
Scrappie. I am twelve years old. I work with Red
Mule except when I go to school. When Red Mule
gets gardens and truck patches to plow in
Blakesburg, he does the plowing and I ride the
disk harrow and work up the ground. Red Mule
is too big to ride the disk harrow.

Is there any place in this country that needs
good mules? Don't you have something for mules
that tractors and trucks can't do? Red Mule and I
were having a hard time making enough money
to buy hay for these mules until Dad rented us
pasture and then gave us his meadows on another farm to cut for hay. I'm helping pay for the
mule pasture by working in Dad's store when

there isn't any school and when Red Mule doesn't need me to help him on a job where we use a mule team. We cut the meadows, rake the hay, and haul it to the barn, and my father gives us half of the hay to feed our mules next winter.

Mister President, mules don't like to eat all the time. Mules like to work. So we must find something for our mules to do. Will you let us know if there is anything they can do that trucks and tractors can't?

If you can think of anything, let me know. Red Mule and I will appreciate it. The mules need help.

Very sincerely,
Frank Lykins, III

Through May and June and into July Scrappie and Red Mule mowed, raked, and hauled hay. Every day Scrappie's mother drove to the farm to see how he and Red Mule were coming along with the work. Often Frank Lykins left the store and drove out to the farm with his wife to see their son. Scrappie was bronzed because he worked bareheaded and without a shirt in the sun. The muscles in his arms and chest were getting bigger. The country life was good for him and his mother and father were as proud of the mules as Scrappie and Red Mule were.

Frank and Mary Lykins had found a new interest in their farm. Now it was more than an investment to them. Their son loved the farm and he had taught them to love it, too. For the first time, they had seen the beauty in a hayfield. They had driven out in the afternoons about sunset while Scrappie and Red Mule were still working. They had stood and looked at the little shocks of golden-brown hay that Scrappie and Red Mule had cut and raked and stacked. Now these little stacks were ready to haul to the barn. In the last rays of the setting sun, all these golden haystacks were a beautiful sight that excited Scrappie's parents.

By the middle of July, Red Mule and Scrappie had two barns filled and were working on filling a third one. One afternoon Scrappie's mother drove out and brought him a letter.

"Scrappie, this letter is from Washington, D.C.," she said. "The envelope says it's from the President!"

Scrappie took the letter and opened it in a hurry. His eyes lit up like stars in the bright July sunlight as he read.

"Oh, Mom, listen to this!" he said. "Let me read it to you! It is from the President of the United States! He's answered my letter! Gee, he must like mules!"

The White House
Washington, D.C.

Frank Lykins, III
Blakesburg, Kentucky

MY DEAR YOUNG FRIEND:

I am very happy to have your letter about mules. I realize you and Red Mule have a problem. Since I have been an Army man, I know mules have come in handy for the Army. They have carried troops and supplies over rough terrain and brought the wounded back. They are useful animals. I have referred your letter to the State Department. You can expect a man any day now, certainly not later than September, to contact you about your mules.

In the meantime, I'll be thinking of other countries, and perhaps parts of our own country, which are undeveloped and where mules are needed. I agree with you, Scrappie; we don't want to lose our mules. We want them here for future generations. I believe there is a place in our civilization and in world civilization for the mule! He has occupied an important and useful place in the development of our great country. My young friend Scrappie, you can believe me, I'll do all I can to help you and Red Mule save the mules.

We'll see if there isn't a place where we can use them. Thank you for writing me.

> Very sincerely,
> Dwight D. Eisenhower
> *President of the United States*

"Gee, Mom, what about it!" Scrappie said happily. "Here, take this letter and keep it for me! Think of the President writing me a letter! We mustn't tell Red Mule or Dad. Let this man come and surprise them!"

"I think that will be wonderful, Scrappie," his mother answered.

Then Scrappie went back to work shocking hay because Red Mule was raking up big windrows with the mule-drawn rake. His mother stood for a few minutes and watched his small brown arms move like pistons as he lifted forkfuls of bright, sweet-smelling hay into the stack.

One afternoon in early August when Scrappie and Red Mule were cutting an alfalfa meadow for the third time, Scrappie's father and mother drove out to see the hay stacks on the meadow in the sunset. As they stood there, another car drove up and stopped near the barn where Scrappie and Red Mule slept while they were cutting hay. A man got out and started walking toward the hayfield. He walked up to where Frank and Mary were standing.

"Can you tell me where I can find a boy by the name of Scrappie Lykins?" he asked. "I inquired at a gas station in Blakesburg and I was directed out here."

The stranger had graying temples and pink cheeks, and wore a tan suit and a soft gray hat. He was smoking a cigar and carried a briefcase.

"Sure, I can tell you where you can find him," Frank Lykins told him. "That's him—the boy right out there stacking the hay. He's our son!"

"Well, Mr. Lykins, I'm glad to know you," the stranger said, extending his hand. "I'm Howard Riggins. I work for the United States Government."

"This is my wife, Mary," Frank Lykins said, looking the stranger over.

"I suppose that letter your son wrote to the President of the United States made you very happy," Howard Riggins told them. "It really brought results!"

"I didn't know my son wrote the President a letter!" Frank Lykins said, with surprise. "I didn't know a thing about it!"

"Well, he did," Mr. Riggins said. "He wrote a letter asking the President what he could do to help him and somebody called Red Mule. The letter was transferred to us. So here I am. Now, where is Red Mule?"

"That's Red Mule out there on that rake," Frank Lykins said. "They're working to save hay for their mules this winter!"

"Would you mind calling both of them over here?" Mr. Riggins asked.

Then Frank Lykins called for Scrappie to come over. With a sweep of his hand, he motioned for Red Mule to come, too.

When Scrappie walked up, his mother said, "Scrappie, this is Mr. Howard Riggins."

"Glad to meet you," Scrappie said.

"And this is Red Mule," Mr. Lykins said, as Mr. Riggins looked big Red Mule over from head to foot.

"Very glad to know you, Red Mule," he said.

"The same to you," Red Mule answered. He sighed as he looked back across the big meadow of sun-cured alfalfa, which was very pretty in the sunset. "Say, that's a pretty field of hay, ain't it!"

"Yes it is," Mr. Riggins answered. "What are you fellows going to feed that pretty hay to?"

"Mules," Scrappie said. "We've got thirty-seven mules, and before the end of this month we'll have fifty."

"That's my business here," Howard Riggins said. "Scrappie, that letter you wrote the President got some action!"

"Shucks, Scrappie, did you write the President?" Red Mule asked.

"Yes, I sure did," Scrappie replied.

"I've come to look over your mules," Mr. Riggins told them. "We pay top prices for strong, healthy mules between the ages of three and six!"

"All of ours but two, Dick and Dinah, are between three and six," Red Mule said. "And Dick and Dinah are not for sale anyway. Not one of our mules has a blemish on him. They are as sound as silver dollars."

"If your mules are sound and young, as you say, I'll take all of them," Mr. Riggins said. "And I'll take a lot more when you buy them up and let me know."

"Say, what do you know about this?" Frank Lykins said. His face was beaming. "Scrappie, how did you ever think to write the President?"

"Well, I read something in a newspaper one evening about the United States sending mules to Turkey," Scrappie explained. "But the paper didn't say who was in charge of the buying. So I wrote to the President to find out!"

"Scrappie, I would never have thought of doing that," Red Mule said, grinning until he showed his big teeth. "You're smarter than I thought! But I always thought you'd do something for mules!"

Scrappie's face lit up with joy. He was happy and his mother was happy, too. She looked at her son and smiled.

"I'll take a shipment of mules this month,"

Howard Riggins said. "I'm staying at the Central Hotel in Blakesburg and I'd like to see your mules tomorrow. Later I'll buy as many as you can get and put in good condition. The Government has plans for mules in a number of countries."

"Gee," Scrappie said. "Where'll we find 'em?"

"Boys, that's business," Frank Lykins said as he pulled his son over close and put his arm around him. "Scrappie, you and your partner have licked this mule problem! You've found something they can do! You've got the problem solved!"

"Red Mule, you'll be sleeping on a feather bed again," Scrappie said.

"We've got to save more mules first," Red Mule said. "Then we can talk about sleep."

Then Red Mule grinned as broadly as he had the day he threw the clods up into the maple tree. He showed all of his big teeth behind his long red beard. Scrappie smiled, too, as the August evening wind blew across the meadow and tousled his long, uncombed hair. Dick and Dinah pawed the meadow dirt with their forefeet and Dick brayed.

"Dick's telling me to come back to 'em, Mr. Riggins," Red Mule said. "We'll see you in the morning and show you our mules. Right now I must get back to Dick and Dinah!"